796.332 Italia, Bob,
It   The Miami
c,1   Dolphins

298/1648   3-114398

DATE DUE

CAVETT ELEMENTARY
LIBRARY

Inside the NFL

THE
MIAMI
DOLPHINS

BOB ITALIA
ABDO & Daughters

Published by Abdo & Daughters, 4940 Viking Drive, Suite 622, Edina, Minnesota 55435.

Copyright © 1996 by Abdo Consulting Group, Inc., Pentagon Tower, P.O. Box 36036, Minneapolis, Minnesota 55435 USA. International copyrights reserved in all countries. No part of this book may be reproduced in any form without written permission from the publisher.

Printed in the United States.

Cover Photo credits: Wide World Photos/Allsport
Interior Photo credits: Wide World Photos

Edited by Kal Gronvall

Library of Congress Cataloging-in-Publication

Italia, Bob, 1955—
      Miami Dolphins / Bob Italia.
        p.   cm. -- (Inside the NFL)
Includes index.
Summary: Describes the past accomplishments and possible future of this football team with a relatively short history.
      ISBN 1-56239-460-6
1. Miami Dolphins (Football team) --History--Juvenile literature. [1. Miami Dolphins (Football team) 2. Football --History.] I. Title. II. Series: Italia, Bob, 1955— Inside the NFL.
GV956.M47I83   1995
796.332'64'09759381--dc20   95-14302
                                                                                   CIP
                                                                                  AC

CONTENTS

A Short but Rich History 4

Joe Robbie 6

A Slow Start 7

Coach Shula 9

Overtime History 10

Perfection 12

Lost Dynasty 14

Dan Marino and the Killer B's 17

Into the 1990s 23

Shula Surpasses Halas 24

Dan vs. Joe 27

One More Championship? 28

Glossary 29

Index 31

A Short but Rich History

For a team with a short NFL history, the Miami Dolphins have accomplished more than most teams with long football traditions.

Miami was one of a few teams to win back-to-back Super Bowl championships. Its coach, Don Shula, holds the NFL record for most career victories. The 1972 Miami Dolphin team is the only club in modern times to go undefeated through an entire season.

Some of the NFL's best offensive players have worn Miami Dolphin jerseys. Larry Csonka, Jim Kiick, Bob Griese, and Mercury Morris all have starred for the Dolphins.

Miami Dolphin coach, Don Shula (L) and managing partner Joe Robbie give a press conference, 1974.

But Miami also has assembled some of the best defensive squads ever. The "No Name" defense helped the Dolphins to their undefeated season and back-to-back championships. And the "Killer B's" nearly won a championship years later.

Ironically, Dan Marino, their best-ever quarterback, still has yet to win a Super Bowl championship. But at 34 years of age, Marino has showed no signs of slowing down his assault on the NFL passing records. Should the Dolphins assemble another killer defense, the Dolphins will add another incredible chapter to their short but incredible history.

Miami quarterback Bob Griese hands off to Larry Csonka, 1974.

Joe Robbie

Joe Robbie was the 50-year-old son of Lebanese and Irish parents. He was also a successful lawyer, and wanted to own a football team in Miami. So Robbie had to persuade American Football League (AFL) officials that they needed a team in southern Florida.

In 1966, Robbie finally got what he wanted—an AFL franchise. All he needed was some players, a coach—and a team name.

To name his team, Robbie held a contest for the fans. There were all kinds of suggestions: Mariners, Marauders, Mustangs, Missiles, Moons, Sharks, and Suns. Six hundred twenty-two Miami fans voted for the name "Dolphins."

"The dolphin is one of the fastest and smartest creatures of the sea," Joe Robbie said. "Dolphins can attack and kill a shark or a whale. Sailors say bad luck will come to anyone who harms one of them."

Choosing a name was one thing. Choosing players who could win was another task altogether. Most AFL teams had players who were not good enough to play in the NFL. The Dolphins were no exception.

Their roster included names like Billy Joe, Laverne Torczon, and Wahoo McDaniel. Rick Norton, George Wilson, and Dick Wood battled for the starting quarterback job. Joe Auer, Bill Hunter, Gene Mingo, and Sam Price played in the backfield. Al Dotson, Tom Nomina, and Rich Zecher anchored the defensive line. Despite the lack of big-name stars, football fans in Miami were happy to have a team.

A Slow Start

No one expected Miami to do well in 1966. The Dolphins had problems at almost every position—especially at quarterback. Eddie Wilson hurt a knee in training camp and missed the season. Dick Wood had little left in his throwing arm, and rookie Rick Norton went out with a fractured jaw in midseason. That left the coach's son, George Wilson, Jr., at quarterback. But coach Wilson signed John Stofa from the North American Football League for the last few games. Stofa came through with four touchdown passes in the season-ending victory over the Houston Oilers. But the Dolphins finished with a 3-11 record.

In 1967, Miami finished fourth with a 4-10 record. The only bright spot was rookie quarterback Bob Griese, who often hooked up with rookie tight end Jack Clancy.

In 1968, the Dolphins added fullback Larry Csonka. Although Csonka looked shaky at times, Wilson could see that his power runner would one day become a star. But Csonka suffered a concussion his first year, and it looked like the big fullback might not return. But Csonka had a special helmet designed that used water pouches to protect his head.

Wilson also signed some of the Dolphins' best players, including running backs Jim Kiick and Mercury Morris, linebacker Nick Buoniconti, offensive guard Larry Little, and defensive end Manny Fernandez. The team was beginning to take shape.

Bob Griese, quarterback for the Dolphins, 1972.

Coach Shula

The Dolphins improved, but very slowly. In 1969, they finished with a 3-10 record and had yet to have a winning season. Robbie decided his team needed a coaching change. He wanted someone who came from a winning tradition. That man was 40-year-old Don Shula.

Shula was the former head coach of the Baltimore Colts for seven years. During that time, he never had a losing season. Most people did not give Robbie much of a chance to sign Shula. After all, Miami was in the more lightly regarded AFL. Shula had been a success in the more respected NFL. But Shula's team had just lost Super Bowl III to the AFL's New York Jets. The Colts were embarrassed with the result. They, too, felt it was time for a coaching change. Moving to Miami sounded wonderful to Shula.

But Shula came to Miami with a heavy price. To compensate the Colts for losing their head coach, NFL commissioner Pete Rozelle awarded Baltimore the Dolphins' 1971 first-round draft pick.

Shula looked forward to the new challenge. And the Dolphins were a challenge. Getting a winning season from them was his first goal. To do that, Shula determined the Dolphins needed to develop disciplined work habits.

At their training camp, the Dolphins had four workouts a day—two in the morning, one in the afternoon, and one in the evening. The hard work eventually paid off. In Shula's first season, the Dolphins ended the season with a 6-game winning streak and finished with a 10-4 record. In the playoffs, however, they lost to the Oakland Raiders, 21-14.

The following season, Miami won the Eastern Division with a 10-3-1 record. Bob Griese became one of the NFL's top quarterbacks. And placekicker Garo Yepremian was the league's top scorer.

Overtime History

In the playoffs, the Dolphins and the Kansas City Chiefs played one of the most exciting games in NFL history. The Chiefs jumped out to a 10-0 lead. But Csonka's touchdown run and Yepremian's field goal tied the score by halftime. In the second half, the Chiefs grabbed the lead once again. But the Dolphins battled back to tie the game.

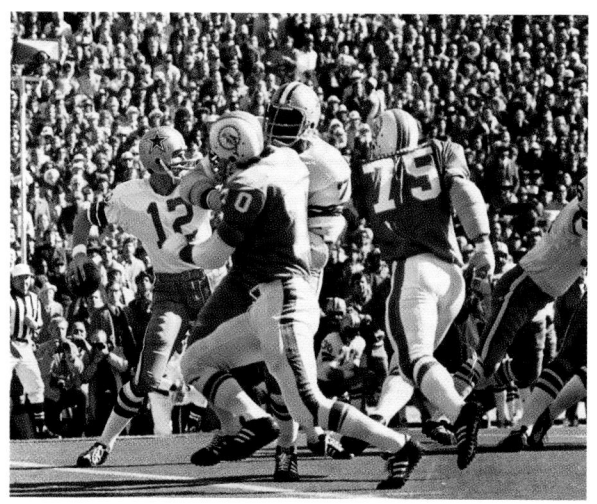

Miami's defense rushes Dallas quarterback Roger Staubach.

With 35 seconds remaining in the game, the Chiefs' Pro Bowl placekicker, Jan Stenerud, trotted onto the field to attempt the game-winning field goal. Stenerud did not miss very often—but this time, his kick sailed wide of the uprights. The game remained tied 24-24, and went into sudden-death overtime.

The defenses dominated the first overtime period and neither team could score. So the game went into a second overtime.

Halfway through the period, Csonka found and opening in the Kansas City line and rumbled for a 29-yard gain that put Miami within field goal range. Yepremian came on to kick a 37-yarder. He would not let his teammates down. His kick split the uprights, and the Dolphins edged Kansas City 27-24 in the longest football game ever.

In the AFC championship game, the Dolphins had a much easier time with Baltimore. Miami pounded the Colts 21-0 to advance to Super Bowl VI.

The Dolphins battled the Dallas Cowboys. Dallas took a 3-0 first-quarter lead, then went up 10-0 in the second quarter on a Roger Staubach touchdown pass. Miami finally got on the board before halftime with a 31-yard Yepremian field goal.

It did not get any better in the second half. The Cowboys scored a third-quarter touchdown to take a 17-3 lead, then tacked on a fourth-quarter score for a commanding 24-3 advantage.

Meanwhile, the Cowboys' Doomsday Defense shut down Griese, Csonka, and the Dolphins. Griese threw for only 134 yards and had one pass intercepted. Csonka rushed 9 times for 40 yards as the offense never got going. Miami lost 24-3.

The 1971 season had been a success. But Shula was not happy. He wanted to win a Super Bowl championship. The 1972 Dolphins not only would win the championship, they would do it in a way that no other team in NFL history had ever accomplished.

Miami field goal kicker Garo Yepremian follows through as the ball heads for the goal posts in Super Bowl VI.

Perfection

The 1972 season was a magical one. On offense, Mercury Morris and Larry Csonka each rushed for more than 1,000 yards—the first rushing duo to accomplish this feat. The Dolphins also had the NFL's number-one-rated defense known as the "No Name Defense" because they did not have well-known defensive stars. Even after Bob Griese broke his leg in the fifth game, backup quarterback Earl Morrall came on to lead the AFC in passing.

But the big story for the 1972 Dolphins was their record. They finished the season at 14-0, the first perfect season since the Chicago Bears racked up a 11-0 record in 1942.

The perfect Dolphins were favored to win their first Super Bowl. But in their first playoff game, Miami barely slipped by Cleveland 20-14. In the AFC championship game against the Steelers, the Dolphins struggled with Pittsburgh before finally winning 21-17. But although the Dolphins were headed to the Super Bowl for the second straight year, they were considered underdogs to the Washington Redskins. One last game separated the Dolphins from perfection. They were not about to let their fans—or themselves—down.

Griese started for the Dolphins after missing 12 games and came out firing. Early in the game, he tossed a 28-yard touchdown pass to Howard Twilley as the Dolphins grabbed a 7-0 lead.

Then the game settled into a defensive battle. As time wore on, the defense intercepted two passes to stop Redskins' drives. When the game finally ended, Miami had a 14-7 victory. The Dolphins were still perfect—and they had won their first world championship. Shula called the 1972 Dolphins the finest team he had ever seen. Nobody had ever done what his team had done.

Larry Csonka (39) crashes over Viking cornerback Bobby Bryant.

The next year, the Dolphins wanted to prove that their magical 1972 season was no fluke. They finished with a 12-2 record and won the Eastern Division for the third year in a row. In the playoffs, they handily defeated Cincinnati 34-16, then took care of Oakland in the AFC championship game to earn a return trip to the Super Bowl.

This time, Csonka was the star. He blasted through the Minnesota Vikings' front line at will and gained a Super Bowl-record 145 yards rushing as the Dolphins won 24-7. Csonka was so successful, Griese spent most of the game handing off to his burly fullback. When it was all over, the Dolphins had joined the Green Bay Packers as the only other team in NFL history to win back-to-back Super Bowls.

Lost Dynasty

The Dolphins had put together a team that could build a dynasty. But the almighty dollar won out over loyalty to the team and fans. In 1974, Paul Warfield, Jim Kiick and Larry Csonka signed with the new World Football League (WFL) for more money. The Dolphins would never be the same. Mercury Morris and Bob Griese were still with the team, but Griese was getting old and could not perform as he once did.

With all the defections, Miami still remained a winning team throughout the 1970s. But in 1975, Shula's Dolphins missed the playoffs for the first time. They would not return to postseason play until 1978. But then, as a wildcard team, Miami lost to Houston 17-9.

The Dolphins brought an old warrior back into the fold in 1979. Csonka returned for a last hurrah and helped Miami to a 10-6 record—good for another division championship. But these Dolphins were not the championship-caliber team they once were. After Miami lost in the playoffs, Csonka decided to retire after an outstanding 11-year career.

In 1980, the last star player from Miami's Super Bowl days saw his career slipping away. Bob Griese was benched in favor of David Woodley and Don Strock. At the end of the season, Griese said goodbye to professional football.

By 1982, Woodley earned the starting quarterback job. In a strike-shortened season, he led the Dolphins to a 7-2 record. In the playoffs, Miami defeated New England 28-13, then beat the New York Jets 14-0 in the AFC championship game. Suddenly, the Dolphins found themselves in the Super Bowl for the fourth time.

Bob Griese scrambles to find a receiver.

Redskins running back John Riggins is gang tackled by the Dolphin defense in Super Bowl XVII.

The Dolphins played the Washington Redskins in Super Bowl XVII. Miami seized the first-quarter lead when Woodley threw a 76-yard touchdown pass to Jimmy Cefalo. By halftime, Miami held on to a 17-10 lead. But they would not score the rest of the game. Led by running back John Riggins, Washington scored 17 second-half points and won 27-17.

Dan Marino and the Killer B's

Though Woodley was playing well, Shula had the chance to draft an outstanding college quarterback from the University of Pittsburgh. His name was Dan Marino.

Beginning his senior year, Marino was a contender for the Heisman Trophy. But he did not perform well as his touchdown production dropped. Most teams did not want to take a chance on him.

Shula, however, did, and made Marino the fifth quarterback chosen in the 1983 draft. Most experts thought it would take Marino years to develop into a starting quarterback. But in the sixth game of the season, Marino took over for Woodley. He won his first four starts—including a 322-yard game against Buffalo.

By the end of his rookie year, Marino's passing statistics were better than Denver's John Elway, whom many thought was the best rookie quarterback in the league.

On the strength of Marino's arm, the Dolphins won 9 of their last 11 games to claim the Eastern Division title. Amazingly, Marino led the AFC in passing. Not only was he named Rookie of the Year, Marino won AFC Offensive Player of the Year honors. And he became the first rookie ever to start in the Pro Bowl.

Quarterback Dan Marino.

MIAMI DOLPHINS

Larry Csonka helps lead Miami to a perfect season in 1972.

In 1966, Joe Robbie forms the Miami Dolphins.

In 1967, Bob Griese joins the Dolphins.

In 1983, Miami selects Dan Marino in the college draft.

Don Shula becomes the NFL's all-time winningest coach in 1994.

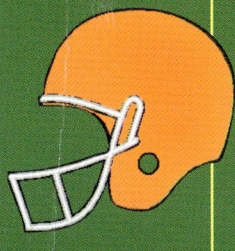

MIAMI DOLPHINS

Coach Don Shula talks to Dolphin quarterback Dan Marino during a timeout.

In 1984, Marino proved to the remaining critics that his 1983 season was no fluke. In Week 5, he passed for 429 yards—breaking Woodley's team record of 408 passing yards in a single game. Later in the season, Marino broke his own record, passing for 470 yards against the Oakland Raiders. In only Game 9, Marino broke Griese's 16-year-old record for most passing yards in one season (2,473).

The Dolphins were a high-scoring offensive machine. They never scored fewer than three touchdowns in a game. Marino led the league in pass attempts, completions, most yards, and most touchdowns.

Marino had plenty of help. Wide receivers Mark Duper and Mark Clayton were named to the Pro Bowl. Clayton set an NFL record with 19 touchdown receptions. Running backs Tony Nathan and Woody Bennett combined for over 1,000 yards rushing.

Miami's defense was just as effective. They had nine defensive players whose last names began with the letter "B." So, the "Killer B's" were born. Doug Betters, Bob Baumhower, Charles Bowser, Jay Brophy, Kim Bokamper, Bob Brudzinski, Mark Brown, and Lyle and Glenn Blackwood made up this tough defensive unit.

In 1984, the Dolphins rolled to an impressive 14-2 mark. In the playoffs, they routed the Seattle Seahawks 31-10, then bounced Pittsburgh 45-28 in the AFC championship game to advance to their fifth Super Bowl. Standing in the way was the San Francisco 49ers and their superstar quarterback, Joe Montana.

It was a dream matchup: two of the league's top quarterbacks going head-to-head. Montana struck first in the first quarter with a touchdown pass, but Marino responded with a touchdown strike of his own. At the end of the first quarter, Miami led 10-7.

Miami Dolphins quarterback Dan Marino passes in Super Bowl XIX against the 49ers.

Dan Marino passes under pressure.

But then the defense failed Miami. San Francisco roared to a 28-16 halftime lead, then shut Marino and the Dolphins out the rest of the way as they won easily 38-16.

In 1985, the Dolphins earned a 12-4 record. Marino's passing numbers fell slightly as he finished fourth in the AFC. Miami made it to the AFC championship game, but lost 31-14 to the New England Patriots.

In 1986, Marino rebounded with 4,746 passing yards and 44 touchdowns—numbers that easily led the AFC. But Marino's impressive passing statistics were not good enough to propel the Dolphins into the playoffs as the team finished with an 8-8 record. In fact, Miami would not return to postseason play until the 1990s.

Into the 1990s

In 1990, 73-year-old owner Joe Robbie died on January 7. Robbie's family took over the team. The Dolphins came within one game of winning the division as they finished 12-4. In the playoffs, the Dolphins won their first-round game against Kansas City, 17-16. But in the second round, Marino got into a shooting match with Buffalo's Jim Kelly. Kelly won the duel 44-34.

Marino was the star again in 1991. He had 25 touchdown passes and 3,970 yards passing. Mark Duper and Mark Clayton each caught 70 passes for over 1,000 yards and 17 touchdowns combined. But the Dolphins did not have a defense. They ranked 25th overall and 27th against the rush, allowing 21.8 points per game. Even though they salvaged an 8-8 record, they finished out of the playoffs for the fifth time in six seasons.

Shula decided Miami needed some changes. Free-agent Keith Jackson joined the team and gave Marino another receiver in his arsenal. The Dolphins also found a defense with new stars such as Troy Vincent, Marco Coleman, and Bryan Cox. The Dolphins started fast with a 6-0 record and won their first division title since 1985. Even more, they won their first playoff game in seven years, shutting out San Diego before falling to the AFC champion Buffalo Bills. Shula got his 300th victory in Week 16, and was less than a full season away from catching George Halas on the career victories list.

Shula Surpasses Halas

Don Shula began the 1993 season saying he wanted the coaching record for most victories to come in a season in which the Dolphins achieved success. But that didn't happen. With a 9-2 record on Thanksgiving Day, the Dolphins had the best record in the NFL. Then they lost their final five games to miss the playoffs. Marino, who hadn't missed a game in eight years, suffered a torn Achilles tendon in the fifth game and was gone. Scott Mitchell took over and was the NFL's Player of the Month of October. Then he too was injured. That left rookie Doug Pederson and Steve DeBerg in charge until Mitchell returned. But the Dolphins could not overcome Marino's loss.

Despite the disappointing season, Shula could finally celebrate his personal accomplishments. Shula got his 325th victory on November 14 to break George Halas' record of 324 career wins.

Marino was healthy again in 1994. In his very first game, he threw for 473 yards in a 39-35 victory over the New England Patriots. The Dolphins jumped out to a 3-0 record. By October 31, the Dolphins were 6-2, good enough for a one-game lead in the AFC East.

On December 4, Miami faced a crucial game against defending AFC champion Buffalo in Miami. A win would hurt the Bills chances at repeating as champions. But Buffalo surprised the Dolphins with a 42-31 victory to pull within one game of Miami.

**Opposite page:
Don Shula celebrates his record-setting game.**

The following week, the Dolphins faced the Kansas City Chiefs. Miami regrouped and won convincingly 45-28, wrapping up a playoff berth. Shula coached his team to victory on a golf cart. Recovering from surgery to repair a ruptured Achilles tendon, Shula kept his leg elevated as he was driven up and down the sideline by an aide. Now all the Dolphins needed was one more win to clinch the division title.

Dolphins receiver Mark Clayton gets away from a Chicago Bear defender while running through the snow.

In Week 16, the Indianapolis Colts surprised the Dolphins with a 10-6 victory. The loss marked the first time in 34 games the Dolphins did not score a touchdown. It also kept Miami from clinching the AFC East. Now the entire season would come down to a game against the Detroit Lions and their star running back, Barry Sanders.

In that game, the Dolphins wrapped up Sanders and the AFC East championship with a 27-20 victory. Running back Bernie Parmalee was the star for Miami as he scored three touchdowns. The Dolphins defense held Sanders, the NFL's leading rusher, to 52 yards on 12 carries.

Miami shared first place with the New England Patriots, but earned the division title by beating the Patriots twice during the regular season. The Marino-led offense finished first in the NFL. Now the Dolphins would host the Kansas City Chiefs and Joe Montana in the first round of the playoffs.

Dan vs. Joe

In a shootout between two of the game's greatest quarterbacks, Marino threw for two touchdowns, and the Dolphins capitalized on a pair of late turnovers to beat Kansas City 27-17. Marino completed 22 of 29 passes for 257 yards and no interceptions. Marino's one-yard touchdown toss to Ronnie Williams tied the game at 17-17 right before halftime. His seven-yard scoring pass to Irving Fryar made it 24-17 in the third quarter. The Dolphins defense held Montana in check in the fourth quarter to preserve the win. Now they would play the Chargers in the AFC championship game in San Diego.

Miami owned the game in the first half as they jumped out to a 21-6 lead. But they had the ball for only 7 minutes and 22 seconds in the second half and didn't score.

Trailing 22-21 late in the fourth quarter, Marino moved the Dolphins to the San Diego 30. But Pete Stoyanovich missed a 48-yard field goal with one second remaining, ending the Dolphins Super Bowl chances.

Marino was 24-of-38 for 262 yards with three touchdowns. After the game, Miami fans wondered if Marino would be back. Though the 33-year-old quarterback was disappointed with the season, he still wanted to win that elusive Super Bowl championship.

One More Championship?

Marino still has his chances to help win an NFL championship for Miami. But Shula and the Dolphins know it will take more than Marino's great arm to lift them to the top. All they need to look at is their incredible 1972 season when the "No Name" defense helped make NFL history. Once the Dolphins assemble a killer defense, Miami will be a champion once again.

GLOSSARY

ALL-PRO—A player who is voted to the Pro Bowl.
BACKFIELD—Players whose position is behind the line of scrimmage.
CORNERBACK—Either of two defensive halfbacks stationed a short distance behind the linebackers and relatively near the sidelines.
DEFENSIVE END—A defensive player who plays on the end of the line and often next to the defensive tackle.
DEFENSIVE TACKLE—A defensive player who plays on the line and between the guard and end.
ELIGIBLE—A player who is qualified to be voted into the Hall of Fame.
END ZONE—The area on either end of a football field where players score touchdowns.
EXTRA POINT—The additional one-point score added after a player makes a touchdown. Teams earn extra points if the placekicker kicks the ball through the uprights of the goalpost, or if an offensive player crosses the goal line with the football before being tackled.
FIELD GOAL—A three-point score awarded when a placekicker kicks the ball through the uprights of the goalpost.
FULLBACK—An offensive player who often lines up farthest behind the front line.
FUMBLE—When a player loses control of the football.
GUARD—An offensive lineman who plays between the tackles and center.
GROUND GAME—The running game.
HALFBACK—An offensive player whose position is behind the line of scrimmage.
HALFTIME—The time period between the second and third quarters of a football game.
INTERCEPTION—When a defensive player catches a pass from an offensive player.
KICK RETURNER—An offensive player who returns kickoffs.
LINEBACKER—A defensive player whose position is behind the line of scrimmage.
LINEMAN—An offensive or defensive player who plays on the line of scrimmage.
PASS—To throw the ball.
PASS RECEIVER—An offensive player who runs pass routes and catches passes.
PLACEKICKER—An offensive player who kicks extra points and field goals. The placekicker also kicks the ball from a tee to the opponent after his team has scored.

PLAYOFFS—The postseason games played amongst the division winners and wild card teams which determines the Super Bowl champion.

PRO BOWL—The postseason All-Star game which showcases the NFL's best players.

PUNT—To kick the ball to the opponent.

QUARTER—One of four 15-minute time periods that makes up a football game.

QUARTERBACK—The backfield player who usually calls the signals for the plays.

REGULAR SEASON—The games played after the preseason and before the playoffs.

ROOKIE—A first-year player.

RUNNING BACK—A backfield player who usually runs with the ball.

RUSH—To run with the football.

SACK—To tackle the quarterback behind the line of scrimmage.

SAFETY—A defensive back who plays behind the linemen and linebackers. Also, two points awarded for tackling an offensive player in his own end zone when he's carrying the ball.

SPECIAL TEAMS—Squads of football players that perform special tasks (for example, kickoff team and punt-return team).

SPONSOR—A person or company that finances a football team.

SUPER BOWL—The NFL Championship game played between the AFC champion and the NFC champion.

T FORMATION—An offensive formation in which the fullback lines up behind the center and quarterback with one halfback stationed on each side of the fullback.

TACKLE—An offensive or defensive lineman who plays between the ends and the guards.

TAILBACK—The offensive back farthest from the line of scrimmage.

TIGHT END—An offensive lineman who is stationed next to the tackles, and who usually blocks or catches passes.

TOUCHDOWN—When one team crosses the goal line of the other team's end zone. A touchdown is worth six points.

TURNOVER—To turn the ball over to an opponent either by a fumble, an interception, or on downs.

UNDERDOG—The team that is picked to lose the game.

WIDE RECEIVER—An offensive player who is stationed relatively close to the sidelines and who usually catches passes.

WILD CARD—A team that makes the playoffs without winning its division.

ZONE PASS DEFENSE—A pass defense method where defensive backs defend a certain area of the playing field rather than individual pass receivers.

INDEX

A

American Football League 6, 7
Auer, Joe 6

B

Baltimore Colts 9
Baumhower, Bob 21
Bennett, Woody 20
Betters, Doug 21
Blackwood, Glenn 21
Blackwood, Lyle 21
Bokamper, Kim 21
Bowser, Charles 21
Brophy, Jay 21
Brown, Mark 21
Brudzinski, Bob 21
Buoniconti, Nick 7

C

Cefalo, Jimmy 16
Clancy, Jack 7
Clayton, Mark 20, 23
Coleman, Marco 23
Cox, Bryan 23
Csonka, Larry 4, 7, 10, 11, 12, 13, 14

D

Dallas Cowboys 11
DeBerg, Steve 24
"Doomsday Defense" 11
Dotson, Al 6
Duper, Mark 20, 23

E

Eastern Division 17
Elway, John 17

F

Fernandez, Manny 7

G

Griese, Bob 4, 7, 9, 11, 12, 13, 14, 20

H

Halas, George 23, 24, 26
Heisman Trophy 17
Hunter, Bill 6

J

Jackson, Keith 23
Joe, Billy 6

K

Kansas City Chiefs 10, 26, 27
Kelly, Jim 23
Kiick, Jim 4, 7, 14
"Killer B's" 4, 21

L

Little, Larry 7

M

Marauders 6
Mariners 6
Marino, Dan 4, 17, 20, 21, 22, 23, 24, 26, 27, 28
McDaniel, Wahoo 6
Mingo, Gene 6
Minnesota Vikings 13
Missiles 6
Mitchell, Scott 24
Montana, Joe 21, 26, 27
Morris, Mercury 4, 7, 12, 14
Mustangs 6

31

N

Nathan, Tony 20
New England Patriots 24, 26
NFL 4, 6, 20, 24, 26, 28
"No Name" defense 4, 28
Nomina, Tom 6
Norton, Rick 6, 7

O

Oakland Raiders 9

P

Parmalee, Bernie 26
Pederson, Doug 24
Player of the Year 17
playoffs 14, 21, 23, 24, 26
Price, Sam 6
Pro Bowl 17

R

Riggins, John 16
Robbie, Joe 6, 9, 23
Rookie of the Year 17
Rozelle, Pete 9

S

San Francisco 49ers 21
Sanders, Barry 26
Sharks 6
Shula, Don 4, 9, 11, 12, 14, 17, 23, 24, 26, 28
Staubach, Roger 11
Stenerud, Jan 10
Stofa, John 7
Stoyanovich, Pete 27
Strock, Don 14
Suns 6
Super Bowl 4, 9, 10, 12, 13, 14, 21, 27

T

Torczon, Laverne 6

V

Vincent, Troy 23

W

Warfield, Paul 14
Washington Redskins 12
Williams, Ronnie 27
Wilson, Eddie 7
Wilson, George 6, 7
Wood, Dick 6, 7
Woodley, David 14, 16, 17, 20
World Football League (WFL) 14

Y

Yepremian, Garo 9-11

Z

Zecher, Rich 6